WHERE IN AMERICA'S PAST

IS CARMEN SANDIEGO?

Text by John Peel

Cover Illustration by Paul Vaccarello

Interior Illustrations by John Nez

Western Publishing Company, Inc.
Racine, Wisconsin 53404

Your Briefing

Congratulations — you've been hired as a rookie detective for the Acme Detective Agency. Your goal is to outsmart Carmen Sandiego and her gang by solving the cases in this book.

There are four cases to solve. Start by removing the cards from the middle of this book. Divide the cards into four groups. You should have the following:

4 Stolen Object Cards
4 Bookmark/Scorecards
8 Suspect Cards
8 Map Cards

Each case involves a stolen object. Decide which case you are going to solve by picking a **stolen object card**. Put the other stolen object cards away until you are ready to solve those cases.

Use a different **scorecard** for each case. As you read through each case, you will be given clues about the suspects. Write these clues down on your scorecard. Compare these clues to your **suspect cards**. Only one suspect will fit all the clues. Once you have picked a suspect, set aside the other cards until the next game.

Each time you are told to go to a different number in the case, mark your **scorecard**. These are your travel points.

When you go to a new number, you may use the **scorecard as a bookmark** to hold your place while you're investigating — sometimes you will have to retrace your steps.

Use the **map cards** for information about the various places that you'll have to visit while tracking down a suspect.

HOW TO SCORE THE GAME:

To win, you must solve the case by finding the right suspect in the right place. You cannot win if you capture the wrong suspect. Once you've found the crook and the stolen object, add up your **total travel points**. Check this score on the last page to see if you've earned a promotion. You earn a promotion by capturing the crook and stolen object in as few moves as possible. The lower your total number of travel points, the more chances you have of earning a promotion.

Ready? Okay — put on your raincoat and hat and get ready to set off on a dangerous mission into America's past for the Acme Detective Agency.

It's your night off, and you're all set to enjoy yourself. You've kicked off your shoes, ordered a pizza, and poured yourself a tall, cold glass of soda. Picking up the remote, you click on your TV and fall into your favorite chair with a happy sigh. It's your first day off in a month, and you can't wait to catch the latest episode of your favorite detective series. Sure, it's full of impossible stunts, big fights, macho men, and gorgeous gals, and you know the business isn't like that. But it's fun to imagine that it could be.

The theme music starts up and then is cut off. A newscaster flashes onto the screen. "We interrupt this program for a news bulletin!" he says. Just what you need. The president probably went bowling or something. Now you have to wait for your detective show.

"Carmen Sandiego and seven of her gang of time-tripping treasure-takers have broken out of jail," the newscaster announces. That grabs your attention. Carmen — on the loose again!

The phone rings. It doesn't take a genius to figure out who'll be on the other end. You scoop it up. "Yeah, Chief," you say, "I saw the news. You want me to come in right away?"

"Chief?" asks a puzzled voice. "This is the chef at the pizza parlor. You want anchovies on your order or not?" You tell him to cancel the order — you're expecting a few orders of your own. The phone rings again, and this time it *is* the Chief.

"Get down here at once!" he orders you. "Carmen and her gang don't waste any time — they've already stolen four priceless historic treasures! I've got the files all ready for you."

"I'm on my way," you promise. You can tell it's going to be one of those nights.

When you reach the office, your personal time machine called the Chronoskimmer is waiting for you. Next you leaf through the four file folders and *The Acme Detective's Handbook of American History* that the Chief left on your desk. Which case will you pick first?

If you want to look for:

Ben Franklin's Bifocal Glasses — go to #50
Robert E. Lee's Horse Traveller — go to #100
The Apollo 8 Space Capsule — go to #133
Old New York City — go to #12

The Acme Detective's
Handbook of American History

THE 1660s

During this period, while the original thirteen colonies are bustling, the land from Texas to California is being held by the Spanish.

May, 1660:

Massachusetts forbids the celebration of Christmas.

May, 1661:

The first Bible in America is printed, in the language of the Algonquin Indians.

May 3, 1662:

The colonies of New Haven and Connecticut are joined.

June 24, 1664:

A new colony named New Jersey is created.

September 7, 1664:

The Dutch governor of New Netherland (a Dutch colony in the New World), Peter Stuyvesant, surrenders to the British. The colony is renamed New York.

August 27, 1665:

The first play in America is performed in Virginia, *Ye Bare and Ye Cubb.* The three actors are fined for performing in public.

THE 1760s

1761:

Rhode Island bans all theaters and public plays.

1762:

Louisiana is given to Spain by France in the Treaty of Fontainebleau.

1763:

The Treaty of Paris ends the French and Indian War.

The Ottawa Indians, under Chief Pontiac, attack the fort at Detroit.

1765:

Chocolate is made for the first time in North America by a company that would become known as Baker's. Its chocolate is still popular today.

The Stamp Act is passed, taxing Americans. Though later replaced by a tax on tea, it was a direct cause of the American Revolution in 1776.

1767:

The first planetarium in America is built in Philadelphia.

The first play, *The Prince of Parthia,* is performed in Philadelphia with professional actors.

1769:

The first indoor toilet in America is built.

THE 1860s

April 3, 1860:
The first Pony Express ride occurs.

April 12, 1861:
The Civil War begins when the Confederates (the army of the Southern states of America) fire on Fort Sumter, a stronghold of the Union (the Northern states of America).

July 1–3, 1863:
Over 50,000 men are killed, wounded, or considered missing at Gettysburg, one of the major and bloodiest battles of the Civil War.

November 19, 1863:
President Abraham Lincoln delivers the historic Gettysburg Address.

Roller skates are invented.

April 9, 1865:
General Robert E. Lee signs the surrender of the Confederate army and states, at the Appomattox Court House. The Civil War is over.

April 14, 1865:
Abraham Lincoln becomes the first U.S. president to be assassinated.

May 5, 1865:
The first train robbery occurs.

April 10, 1866:
The ASPCA, the American Society for the

Prevention of Cruelty to Animals, is founded.

1868:

Susan B. Anthony forms a newspaper to promote the equal rights of women and men.

Louisa May Alcott's book *Little Women* is published.

December 10, 1869:

The Wyoming Territory is the first place in the United States that gives women the right to vote.

THE 1960s

1960:

Harper Lee's book *To Kill a Mockingbird* is published.

May 10, 1960:

The first underwater voyage around the world is completed by the submarine *USS Triton*.

November 8, 1960:

John F. Kennedy is elected president.

May 5, 1961:

Astronaut Alan B. Shepard, Jr., becomes the first American to travel in space.

August 13, 1961:
The construction of the Berlin Wall begins.

November 22, 1963:
John F. Kennedy becomes the fourth president of the United States to be assassinated.

January 17, 1966:
Robert C. Weaver becomes the first Black person to hold a Cabinet office.

January 15, 1967:
The first Super Bowl is won by the Green Bay Packers.

October 2, 1967:
Thurgood Marshall becomes the first Black Supreme Court justice.

April 4, 1968:
Dr. Martin Luther King, Jr., is assassinated.

June 5, 1968:
Senator Robert F. Kennedy, the brother of John F. Kennedy, is assassinated.

July 20, 1969:
Astronaut Neil A. Armstrong becomes the first human being to set foot on the Moon.

The Chase

#1. You've arrived in the state of Massachusetts, and the year is 1662. The members of the Congregational Church are about to split into two groups — and you'd better split, too. This is the wrong place and time. Head for #21.

#2. On the quiet shore of the East River in New York City, you find an old Dutch fisherman. You ask about the crook you're chasing.

"Ah," the gray-eyed fisherman replies. "What a strange person. Talked about going to a time when women can vote. It will never happen."

There's no point in telling him he's wrong, so you thank him and hurry back to #14 to check out your clues.

#3. You've reached the state of Arkansas on Election Day, November 6, 1860, and Abraham Lincoln has been elected president. In just a few weeks, the state of South Carolina will drop out of the Union, followed by several other Southern states. Soon the Civil War will break out. You'd better leave before the fighting starts — try #21.

#4. It's December of 1660, and you're in the state of Massachusetts. The Puritans don't believe in celebrating Christmas, so right now the best present you can give yourself is a trip somewhere else. Try #21.

#5. The Chronoskimmer stops, and you find yourself in Virginia. The year is 1960, and it's July 4. This year, for the first time, the American flag has the full fifty stars on it — Alaska and Hawaii both joined the Union in 1959.

Take a break for a Fourth of July picnic while the Chronoskimmer tracks down some clues. Now you have a choice: You can question one of the people listed or you can investigate a place.

If you want to talk to:
A beatnik — go to #79
A Southern Belle — go to #34
A blues singer — go to #127

If you're ready to leave for:
Texas in the year 1969 — go to #163
Arizona in the year 1962 — go to #22
Alabama in the year 1862 — go to #87

#6. You find the small cabin where the Quaker lives and discover him eating breakfast. He asks, "What can I do for thee?" (Sounds funny, but that's how Quakers talk.) You ask him about the man you're after.

"Verily, he was here," the Quaker tells you. "He spoke of visiting the first state to join the Union. But I know of no Union."

You tell him to wait about a hundred years and he will. Then you head back to #23 to check out this new clue.

#7. You've landed in Florida in 1968. The Gator Aide is a young woman who works on an alligator farm. Eyeing the alligators nervously, you ask her if she's seen the crook you're tracking.

She nods. "The villain mentioned something about wanting to see a president just before he's assassinated." She smiles. "You look like you're in good shape — how'd you like to wrestle one of the smaller gators?"

On that note, it's definitely time to head back to #133 and check up on this clue!

#8. You've reached Manheim, Pennsylvania, and the new glass factory of Henry William Stiegel. He's inside, looking glum about his business.

"Don't worry," you tell him. "Someday you'll be a smashing success."

"Don't say smashing in here!" he says with a shiver. "What can I do for you?"

You ask him about the crook you're trailing. "Oh, her." He sighs. "What a strange lady. She asked me about Gettysburg's address. I said I didn't know who Gettysburg was, much less his address. She said it wasn't a person's home but a famous speech by Abraham Lincoln, and that she was going somewhere to read all about it."

Slip back to #41 to check out this new information.

#9. You've landed in Connecticut in 1964. Lyndon B. Johnson became president a few months ago, after John F. Kennedy was assassinated. This year Johnson is running a campaign for reelection. But you've got other things on your mind — like running after a crook.

The Chronoskimmer flashes three clues for you.

If you want to talk to:

A Republican — go to #135
A Democrat — go to #103
A sailor — go to #95

#10. The organ maker's workshop is a mess, with pieces of metal and wood all over. "This fellow needs to get organized," you mutter.

Then you see a man rushing at you, waving a large pipe over his head and screaming.

You jump out of his way, but he keeps running. He slams into a pile of wood and is knocked unconscious. You figure he must be working for Carmen's gang, so you head back to #55 to check out another lead.

#11. So this is Delaware, 1660. The local businessmen aren't very happy about a new law that says they must sell their best goods — like sugar, tobacco, cotton, and wool — only to England. And you're not too happy because you're in the wrong place. Time to head to #21.

#12. The village of Manhattan in old New York City in 1664 is nothing like the sprawling town full of skyscrapers that you're used to seeing. The bustling harbor is full of sailing ships.

Away from the waterfront, much of Manhattan is still open land or farms. Although the city has just changed its name from New Amsterdam to New York, most of the people living here are Dutch.

Your Chronoskimmer buzzes to tell you it has finished collecting leads for you. Now you have a choice: You can question one of the people listed or you can investigate a place.

If you want to speak to:
A Dutch burgher — go to #65
Hans from Harlem — go to #33
Richard Nicholls, the governor
of New York — go to #142

If you're ready to leave for :
Oklahoma in 1969 — go to #98
Michigan in 1861 — go to #166
New Mexico in 1964 — go to #49

#13. You've trailed Della Kitessen to a sandwich shop in New London, Connecticut. The sailors often come here to order submarine sandwiches. But there's no sign of Della, so you'd better sail off to #74.

#14. You've arrived in New York in 1666. The village on Manhattan Island has been here for over fifty years now, but it's still hard to believe that it will someday turn into one of the world's busiest cities.

The Chronoskimmer beeps, telling you to examine these clues. Now you have a choice: You can question one of the people listed or you can investigate a place.

If you want to talk to:
A *farmer* — *go to #63*
A *fisherman* — *go to #2*
A *potter* — *go to #148*

If you're ready to move on to:
Delaware in 1769 — *go to #84*
Illinois in 1969 — *go to #116*
Utah in 1869 — *go to #35*

#15. The bomb shelter salesman is doing brisk business right now. Back at the beginning of the 1960s, things were very tense between the United States and the U.S.S.R. But by 1967 the Cold War has thawed out a bit, and now the salesman is hungry for business.

"What would you like?" the salesman asks.

You explain that you're looking for a crook, and ask if he can help.

"If you're not buying anything, get lost," he tells you.

Well, that was a complete waste of time. With a sigh, you head back to #85 in search of a better lead.

#16. You've arrived in Louisiana in the year 1763. Most of the settlers speak French, but in a treaty last year, France gave this territory to Spain, making the French settlers pretty unhappy. You know that France will get this land back in 1800, and the United States will buy it from France in 1803 in the Louisiana Purchase. But you don't want to tell the locals any of this — it would just confuse them.

Luckily, the computer beeps at you before you start blabbing, and you check out your leads. Now you have a choice: You can question one of the people listed or you can investigate a place.

If you want to talk to:
Marie — go to #45
Trapper Jean — go to #114
Pierre the Bear — go to #162

If you think the crook has fled to:
Hawaii in 1960 — go to #130
Massachusetts in 1660 — go to #4
Colorado in 1867 — go to #73

#17. You find Prudence planting peas in the garden beside her clapboard house. She smiles, and you ask her if she can help you find the man you're looking for.

"He was here a while ago," she tells you. "He was a strange man. He said he was going to a place that's been a U.S. state for more than sixty years. I asked him what a U.S. state was. He told me it is part of a country called the United States. He said its symbol is the bald eagle, his favorite bird. Do you know what he was talking about?"

"He's a crook, ma'am," you tell her. You thank her for the clue and head for #139.

#18. This is New York in 1867. It's dirty, and the streets are narrow and crowded. The first elevated railroad in the United States has just been built here. It's a new way to travel. Speaking of which, you'd better travel to #21.

#19. You've arrived in Kansas, in 1865. This part of the Wild West looks pretty tame right now, though. The Civil War has just ended, and settlers are starting to move westward again. But the towns here are still only a few streets and buildings in the middle of the vast prairie.

The Chronoskimmer has finished collecting clues, and you look them over. Now you have a choice: You can question one of the people listed or you can investigate a place.

If you want to talk to:
Chester — go to *#36*
Lester — go to *#109*
The nester — go to *#169*

If you're ready to move to:
California in 1967 — go to *#85*
Arkansas in 1860 — go to *#3*
Rhode Island in 1968 — go to *#56*

#20. Carl is a guide at the Carlsbad Caverns in the state of New Mexico. As you walk up to him, he begins his tour narration. "These caverns are the deepest underground passageways ever found by man," he tells you. "There are three levels. The first is 754 feet below ground, the second is 900 feet below, and the third is

1,320 feet below. They are also the world's largest known caves, consisting of a total —"

You quickly cut him off. "I need information about the crook I'm after."

"Well, there was a crooked-looking person in my last tour group," he recalls. "Someone with brown hair. Couldn't stand the dripping water down here — wanted to go somewhere where hardly any people had bathrooms in their houses. Seemed like a funny thing to say."

"It takes all sorts," you tell him. Then you head back to #49 to check out this clue.

#21. I'm afraid you've fallen for one of Carmen's red herrings. There's nobody here at all. Return to the last site that gave you a list of leads and follow the thief's trail more carefully this time. **Don't forget to put down a travel point for moving here to #21 and to return to the site with the list of leads.**

#22. You've landed in Arizona, in the year 1962. In October, the U.S.S.R. had threatened to set up atomic missiles in Cuba, not far from U.S. shores. President Kennedy ordered a blockade of Cuba to prevent the Russian missiles from arriving. The world hung on the brink of nuclear war, until the Russians finally backed down.

Meanwhile, you're waiting for the results of your computer's search for clues. Finally, the screen lights up with the information that you need. Now you have a choice: You can question one of the people listed or you can investigate a place.

If you want to interrogate:
Harry Sonar — go to #30
Tombstone Tess — go to #99
The Grand Canyon guide — go to #107

If you're ready to follow the crook to:
Massachusetts in 1662 — go to #1
New Jersey in 1762 — go to #54
Georgia in 1662 — go to #139

#23. It's 1669, and you've reached the colony of New Hampshire. By now there are only about 85,000 European settlers in all of America, and most of them are living in small communities close to the sea.

The Chronoskimmer buzzes. It's ready to give you some information. Now you have a choice: You can question one of the people listed or you can investigate a place.

To talk to:
"Bowling" Greene — go to #59
Nathaniel Morton — go to #132
The Quaker — go to #6

If you think the crook went to:
Vermont in 1968 — go to #92
South Carolina in 1963 — go to #156
Vermont in 1863 — go to #27

#24. You're on a deserted beach that will one day become Miami Beach. Right now, it's a pretty depressing place, especially for you. There's no sign of Lucinda Boltz — after all, there's nothing here for her to repair. You'd better tool on over to #74.

#25. Hawaii has been the background for many TV shows over the years — "Magnum, P.I.," "Hawaii Five-O," and in 1960, "Hawaiian Eye." You arrive at a hotel where they're filming an episode. You see the show's star, a young actor named Robert Conrad, talking to the director.

Then you spot Ike, the man you're after. He sees you and dashes across the set. The director calls for the actors to take their places. On cue,

Robert Conrad turns around and punches Ike. Caught by surprise, Ike collapses. Conrad looks puzzled.

"Hey, thanks for catching one of Carmen Sandiego's gang," you tell him. "Can I have your autograph?"

"Sure," he says. "Got a piece of paper?"

You spot a scrap of paper sticking out of Ike's pocket. It's a list of the names and addresses of Carmen's gang!

If you are after the crook:

Lucinda Boltz — go to #146

Casey Rah Sirah — go to #53

Della Kitessen — go to #150

Skip Tumelu — go to #78

Claire Voyant — go to #110

Homer DeBrave — go to #134

Carmen Sandiego — go to #122

Phil R. Yup — go to #86

#26. You've arrived at a Little League baseball game, where you've had a tip that Homer DeBrave is about to steal home — that is, home plate, for his personal collection! But you've been misled, and there's no one here. You'd better steal on home yourself — to #74.

#27. This is Vermont, and the year is 1863. Roller skates are the newest fad in cities like Chicago and New York, but there aren't many sidewalks here in Vermont to skate on. Better skate over to #21.

#28. The year is 1863. Congress has begun to provide mail delivery in certain cities, including New York. Pat, a recent arrival from Ireland, got a job as one of the first New York City postal carriers. You ask him about the person you're tailing.

"Sure," he tells you in his thick Irish brogue, "I remember that rogue. Has a real sweet tooth — tried to steal my bar of chocolate. When I grabbed it back, the crook vowed to go somewhere to find one."

That doesn't tell you much — or does it? You head back to #89 to check out the possibilities.

#29. You've landed in Virginia, in 1665. Everyone in the town of Acomac has gone to the theater to see *Ye Bare and Ye Cubb*. Unfortunately, three of the actors — all of them local residents — will be arrested for appearing in the play. You can't find anyone to answer your questions, so you have to give up and go to #21.

#30. Harry Sonar of Arizona turns out to be a bit of a crook himself. He's selling metal hats to protect people in case atomic missiles fall in their backyards. What a racket! When you flash your Private Detective badge at him, he falls to his knees, almost in tears.

"Don't run me in," he begs. "I'll be good, I promise."

"There is one thing you can do to help me," you say, and then tell him about the crook you're after.

"Oh, I saw him," he replies quickly. "Said he was going somewhere to celebrate Christmas. In July? He must have been out in the sun too long."

"He can't be that dumb — he didn't fall for your hat trick," you reply. You make him promise to stop his silly hat game. He promises. But as you walk toward #22 to check this clue, you hear his voice behind you.

"Get your protective shoes here! Genuine, radiation-proof shoes!"

#31. You've trailed Claire Voyant to a Conestoga wagon maker located in Lancaster, Pennsylvania. These wagons will transport pioneers to settle out West. But nothing's settled for you, because Claire's not here. You'd better move on out to #74.

#32. You've reached Virginia in the year 1763. The second-oldest college in the United States, the College of William and Mary, has been here for almost seventy years. But you've checked out the student body, and there's nobody here you want to investigate. Better head for #21.

#33. You're in the quiet farm village of Harlem in 1664. The village was named after the town of Haarlem in Holland. You shake hands with Hans, a cheerful young man, and ask about the thief you're after.

"The person said something about an astronaut," he tells you. "What in the world is that?"

"It's a kind of out-of-this-world explorer," you say. Before he asks more questions, you'd better fly back to #12 to check out this clue.

#34. Belle turns out to be a real Southern belle. You ask her about the thief you're after.

"Oh, I sure did meet him," she tells you. "But he had no manners at all. Why, he told me he was off to the place and time of the first train robbery. The very idea! Why, if my boyfriend, Beauregard, ever skedaddled away with such a flimsy excuse —"

You thank her and skedaddle back to #5.

#35. The Chronoskimmer has brought you to Utah in 1869. Two railroads have finally connected at Promontory Point, Utah, on May 10, making it possible to travel coast to coast by train. But your own travels have reached a dead end. Better head off to #21 now.

#36. You arrive at the marshal's office in Dodge City, Kansas. Chester is the handyman. When you tell him you're looking for a thief, he frowns. "Golly, the marshal's out of town right now," he says. "He's got a posse out looking for some cattle rustlers."

"Then maybe you can help me," you say.

"Well, I do recall a very nice lady who moseyed in here. Said she wanted to kill a mockingbird. Sounds kinda silly, don't it? I wouldn't think mockingbirds would taste all that good."

You explain to him that she wanted to buy a book called *To Kill a Mockingbird*. Chester shakes his head and says he's not much for reading. You say goodbye and mosey off to #19.

#37. You've landed in the town of Hartford, Connecticut, in 1865. The *Hartford Daily Courant* is a newspaper that has been in business for a century — and you know that it'll still be in business more than a century later, in your own time. You stop by its offices just as the paper has gone to press. The editor has a few free moments, so you ask him about the woman you're after.

"I remember her," he tells you. "She mentioned that she was going to a state that was once a French colony."

You thank him for his help and hurry back to #118 to check out this clue.

#38. Since Kentucky lies on the border between the Northern and Southern states, some of its natives fight for the Union, others for the Confederacy. It's 1864, and the soldier you've come to see has been wounded in battle. You sit by his bed and ask him if he knows anything about the crook you're after.

"I saw him," the soldier tells you. "He has green eyes, and he mentioned wanting to see a submarine. I've heard of those new underwater boats, but I've never seen one."

You thank him for his help and wish him well. Then you head back to #91.

#39. It's 1862, and you've landed in the middle of the Civil War. The Confederacy's General Stonewall Jackson earned his nickname by never budging in battle, even under the worst gunfire. He's one of Commander General Robert E. Lee's best men. When he hears that you want to see him about the stolen horse, Traveller, Jackson calls you into his tent.

"I trust you will catch the scoundrel who did this," he growls. "One of my men overheard the thief say he was going to a time before any presidents were assassinated. What a fool notion! No president has ever been assassinated."

You don't tell him that President Lincoln will be the first — no use putting ideas into his head. You march back to #100 to check out this clue.

#40. You find the student reading a history book. He's happy to stop studying, though, so you ask him about the crook you're chasing.

"Yes, I saw the woman you're looking for," he tells you. "She said she had to go somewhere where she could spend some Confederate money. She suggested that I give her some good English shillings for it, but I refused."

You really should stay and give him a quick history lesson, but you're in a hurry to reach #145 to check out this new information.

#41. The Chronoskimmer brings you to Philadelphia, Pennsylvania. The year is 1769, and the colonists are getting tired of British rule and the new taxes that have been imposed. As you wait for the Chronoskimmer to track down clues for you, you read a copy of the *Pennsylvania Gazette*. Until recently, the paper was edited by Benjamin Franklin.

The on-board computer finally buzzes to let you know it's ready. Now you have a choice: You can question one of the people listed or you can investigate a place.

If you want to talk to:

George at the forge — go to #61

Henry William Stiegel — go to #8

Prudence the student — go to #126

If you're ready to move on to:

Hawaii in 1965 — go to #82

Connecticut in 1865 — go to #118

Virginia in 1665 — go to #29

#42. You arrive on the banks of Conestoga Creek, in Lancaster, Pennsylvania. It's the year 1760. Engineer Henry Williams is reading a newspaper article about an Englishman named James Watt, who invented an engine run by steam power.

"I've got an idea to build a steam-powered boat," Williams tells you. "Think how fast you could sail to Europe!"

"Not a bad idea," you say. You don't tell him that Robert Fulton will invent a steamship that works.

You ask about the thief you're after. "I'm afraid I can't help you," he admits. You thank him anyway and steam on to #50.

#43. You've arrived in Vermont in the summer of 1968. There are many ski trails in Vermont's beautiful Green Mountains. You meet a ski instructor in Killington. She asks you where your skis are. You admit that the only trail you're interested in is a crook's trail.

"The man you're after didn't like skiing, either," she tells you. "He said he preferred to go see a play."

You thank her for her help and head for #92 to check out this clue.

#44. You've reached Charleston, South Carolina, in the year 1662. English settlers will found the city in eight years, but right now you're all alone in the wilderness. Better head for #21 at once.

#45. You land in Louisiana in the year 1763. Marie lives in one of the most elegant houses in New Orleans, but she's only a kitchen servant. You help her fetch water from the pump and ask about the crook you're chasing.

"Ah, *oui*," she replies in a strong French accent. "She was 'ere. She said she was looking for a Mexican restaurant. I told her we serve only

French and Creole food in this house. Then she say she going to visit a state that 'as just joined the Union."

You thank her for her help, and she curtsies. Then you head back to #16 to check out this clue.

#46. You've reached Michigan in 1862. You're standing on the shore of Lake Michigan, and there's nobody in sight. Better take a trip to #21 to sort it out.

#47. You've tracked Lucinda Boltz to a printer's shop in Philadelphia. But the press has broken down, and the printer has closed up shop. You'd better press on to #74.

#48. The swamp rat is an old man who lives on the edge of a swamp. He sticks a long-bar-reled rifle in your face and glares at you angrily. "You're after my farm!" he yells. "Well, you won't get it, you varmint! I'll blow you clear into next week."

"Calm down," you tell him. "I'm not after your farm, honestly." (You wonder what he farms here — mud?) "I'm a detective and I'm after a thief," you explain.

"Well, why didn't you say so?" he says, pulling the gun away from your face. "She was just here, and if you move quickly you should just about catch her," he says.

Head back to #121 fast and check one of the other leads. You're almost there!

#49. The Chronoskimmer comes to a halt in New Mexico. The year is 1964, and it seems to be a pretty exciting place and time. There's atomic research going on at Los Alamos, plus rocket testing at White Sands.

The on-board computer beeps, and you find it has already lined up some clues for you. Now you have a choice: You can question one of the people listed or you can investigate a place.

If you want to speak to:
The rocket man — go to #102
Carlsbad Carl — go to #20
Atomic Ann — go to #57

If you're ready to move to:
North Carolina in 1669 — go to #158
Pennsylvania in 1869 — go to #106
Pennsylvania in 1769 — go to #41

#50. You've reached Philadelphia, and the year is 1760. You find Benjamin Franklin at his home, scratching his head in despair.

"It's awful," he says. "I had a great idea, you see. With my weak eyes, I needed two different kinds of glasses — one for seeing far-away objects and one for things close up. I got fed up with constantly switching them, so I invented what I call bifocals. To see far away, I look through the top lens; for reading, I look through the bottom lens. But a thief stole my bifocals, so now I have to use two pairs of glasses again."

You check your computer for some leads. Now you have a choice: You can question one of the people listed or you can investigate a place.

If you want to talk with:
Mickey the Finn — go to #70
Betsy Ross — go to #119
Henry Williams — go to #42

If you think the crook went to:
Maine in 1860 — go to #131
Iowa in 1869 — go to #155
Virginia in 1960 — go to #5

#51. You arrive at an iron foundry, one of the main industries in Illinois. The iron man is casting molten iron, a hot and sometimes dangerous job. You wait until he's finished his shift, then you ask about the crook you're chasing.

"Yeah, he was here," the iron man tells you. "Said he was going off to bet on a horse race."

You race back to #116 to check out this clue.

#52. You've arrived in Alaska, and the year is 1960. It's not as cold and bleak as you expected, but it might as well be. You've come to the wrong spot, so head along to #21.

#53. You've tracked Casey Rah Sirah to Waikiki Beach in Hawaii, where you find plenty of sand, sun, and tanned people — but no sign at all of Casey. You'd better head for #74 to find out why.

#54. This is New Jersey, and the year is 1762. Though there's plenty to see and do, none of it is of interest to you. You discover this is the wrong place to be, and you set off to #21.

#55. You've reached Pennsylvania, and the year is 1762. Philadelphia is a center of learning, and an important area during the American Revolution. Even now things are happening.

Your on-board computer is beeping away. It has unearthed these three leads for you.

If you want to talk with:

The organ maker — go to #10
The lamplighter — go to #128
The philosopher — go to #71

#56. You've reached Rhode Island in the year 1968. This is the smallest state in the Union. You feel pretty small yourself when there's no sign of the thief you're chasing. Go to #21.

#57. Atomic Ann is the nickname of one of the scientists at Los Alamos. She's busy splitting atoms, and it has given her a splitting headache. "You're the second person to interrupt me today," she tells you, annoyed.

You apologize and tell her that you're after that other person. You ask if she can tell you anything at all about the thief.

"That pest went off to a planetarium," she says. "Wanted to see the stars."

You thank her and beat a quick retreat. Time

to head back to #49 and check out this clue.

#58. You've trailed Carmen Sandiego to a drive-in theater where the Beatles movie, *A Hard Day's Night,* is playing. But you'd better just call it a hard day, because there's no sign at all of Carmen here. Time to pack it in and go to #74.

#59. "Bowling" Greene is a farmer who enjoys the game of bowls. It's a lot like the modern sport of bowling, except it's played outside instead of in a bowling alley. You offer to help him set up his pins if he can tell you anything about the man you're trailing.

"He was indeed here," Mr. Greene tells you, "but he said he was off to a time when women can vote. Oh, I do recall that he had black hair."

You thank him for his help. He bowls his ball and makes a strike. You roll back to #23 to check out this new information.

#60. You've trailed Casey Rah Sirah to a spot in Florida that will one day become Disney World. Right now though, it could be called

Dismal World, it's so wild and swampy. Even worse, there's no sign of Casey. You decide to give up the trail and head for #74.

#61. You reach the forge where George the blacksmith works. He has been trying a new method for heating iron, using coal. He's still ironing out the details, and he's grumpy.

"Get out of here!" he yells. "You're as bad as that crooked woman who came past here today. I'll tell you just what I told her: Be off with you! I mean it!"

Ducking the lumps of coal he's throwing, you head back to #41.

#62. You find William in the isolated Georgia woods. William is hunting along a small river, and you call out to him.

"Don't see many people in these parts," he says to you. "But you're the second man I've seen today."

"Well, the first man you saw is a thief, and I'm tracking him," you explain. "Can you tell me anything about him?"

William strokes his beard. "He told me he was very fond of eagles. I told him he'd come to the right place, because you can see plenty of birds in these parts. But he didn't stay long."

Neither will you, now that you have a clue. It's time to head back to #139.

#63. The farmer runs a small farm that will one day become part of New York City. Right now, though, it's good pasture land for grazing cattle. You ask him about the man you're trailing.

"Normally I believe in work, not gossiping," the farmer tells you sternly. "But that man was so annoying I couldn't help but notice his gray eyes. Say, do you want to give me a hand milking the cows?"

You explain that you have work of your own to do, and head back to #14 to check out this clue.

#64. Flower power is a big theme in 1967. You find a young girl in San Francisco's Golden Gate Park, sitting cross-legged on the grass, staring at a bunch of tulips.

"Peace," she says, smiling at you.

"Let's hope so," you reply. You ask about the woman you're seeking, and she smiles again.

"She really gave me bad vibrations," she says. "She told me she was going to travel through time to visit the Civil War. It really blew my mind."

You thank her and give her the peace sign. Then you go to #85 to check out the new clue.

#65. You've reached the colony of New York in 1664. The Dutch burgher is a wealthy man who owns a fancy mansion downtown and a pig farm uptown. The burgher is watching his workers feed the pigs when you arrive. "Must be a ham burgher," you mutter.

"Have some respect!" the man says, sniffing. "A burgher is a man of importance, I'll have you know."

You apologize then ask about the thief you're looking for.

"Do I look like the sort of person who keeps company with thieves?" he asks angrily. "Be off with you, or I'll have one of my farmhands take a whip to you!"

There's no point in staying here. So you head back to #12 to follow a better lead.

#66. You've arrived at the Underground Railroad in 1864. It's not really a railroad but a group of people who risked their lives to help slaves escape from the South before and during the Civil War. The best-known member was a slave herself, Harriet Tubman. Many others were white people who were ashamed of the way slaves were treated.

The person you're looking for is an elderly lady. She's suspicious of you, until you explain that you're not looking for slaves, but a thief.

"I recall that man," she says. "He said he was going to visit one of the original thirteen colonies that became one of the first thirteen states." she says.

You thank her and wish her good luck with her work. Then you head back to #91 to check out this information.

#67. You've reached Connecticut in the year 1662. This year the colony has been granted a royal charter, merging it with the colony of New Haven. But it isn't a good haven for you, because no one here knows anything about the thief you are looking for. Head along to #21 to check out what's happening.

#68. This is the year 1665, and you're in Maryland. Here, on the shores of Chesapeake Bay, it's a great place for crabs, but you're beginning to feel crabby yourself. Go to #21 to check out what's wrong.

#69. It's 1963, and you've reached Utah's Monument Valley, a stretch of red desert where many Western films are shot. You are feeling monumentally stupid, because you're in the wrong spot. You'd better hustle over to #21.

#70. You've landed in the colony of Pennslyvania in 1760. Many European immigrants have come to this beautiful rich farmland, including settlers from Finland. One of these Finns is Mickey, a young man who works in a livery stable. You ask him about the crook you're chasing.

"A very odd man." Mickey recalls. "Said he was off to visit one of the original thirteen states. I'm not sure what that meant, though."

"I have a pretty good idea what he meant," you tell him. This will certainly rule out some possible destinations. With this clue head back to #50 and check out the destination leads.

#71. The American Philosophical Society was formed by Benjamin Franklin in 1743. In the library of the building, you find your philosopher quietly reading. Then you notice another man, who's stealing some valuable books from the shelves.

"Hey!" you yell, and rush across the room.

"Quiet!" the philosopher snaps at you.

The crook sees you coming and tries to run for it. The philosopher sighs and calmly sticks out one foot. The crook trips over it crashing to the floor. You jump on him, and in seconds you have him handcuffed.

"Now will you be quiet?" the philosopher asks. "I really must finish this book!"

You see that the crook has a list of names and addresses of Carmen's gang!

If the thief you're hunting is:

Claire Voyant — go to #31
Casey Rah Sirah — go to #152
Della Kitessen — go to #80
Homer DeBrave — go to #168
Phil R. Yup — go to #104
Carmen Sandiego — go to #120
Skip Tumelu — go to #164
Lucinda Boltz — go to #47

#72. You've trailed Homer DeBrave to what will someday be spring training camp for many major league baseball teams. But you're about a century too early, and the place is deserted. You'd better head for #74.

#73. You've landed in 1867, in Denver, the main city in Colorado Territory. Everybody seems to have gold fever, and they're out in the mountains panning for gold nuggets. Since your lead hasn't panned out, head for #21.

#74. Well, you've tracked the thief to the right time and place, but you've picked the wrong suspect. You won't be able to return the treasure this time. That's not the way to become a world-famous detective! Head for the back of the book and add up your score. Because you tried to arrest the wrong person, **add ten points to your travel score. Start this game over, or begin a new game**.

#75. You find Skip Tumelu in Connecticut, where the America's Cup yacht race was just held. He's hiding out in Mystic, an old ship-building town. Skip has ordered a seafood dinner at a restaurant near the wharf. You grab a fishnet off the restaurant wall and drop it over his head.

"I just made the catch of the day," you tell him. Benjamin Franklin's missing bifocals are in his jacket pocket. After Skip is picked up by the police, you call the Chief and report that your case is solved.

"Congratulations," the Chief answers. "Why don't you head for the back of the book to check your score. Maybe you've earned a promotion and a raise!"

#76. The year is 1660, and you've arrived in Georgia. It'll be another seventy-three years before this land becomes a colony. What's more, you've lost track of the crook you're after. Better blaze a trail to #21.

#77. Summer in New York City in 1863 is a wonderful time. Twelve-year-old Ruby is into the latest fad invention — roller skates. In fact, while you talk to her, she skates circles around you. Although you're getting dizzy, you ask about the thief you're following.

"He was here," Ruby calls, skating past you. "Left to go to one of the original thirteen colonies."

Head whirling, you make your way to #89 to check out this new clue.

#78. Skip Tumelu's trail leads you to Hawaii Volcanoes National Park on the island of Hawaii. It's hot here, but the trail is cold. Skip seems to have skipped the place. Time you did, too, and went to #74.

#79. It's 1960, and you find yourself in a smoky jazz club in Virginia. The men in the audience wear little pointy beards, and the women have long hair. Even though the lights are low, people wear dark glasses.

The beatnik you're after sits near the door, eyes closed, snapping his fingers in time to the music. You ask him about the thief you're tracking. He opens his eyes and shakes his head.

"Like, crazy, man," he tells you. "He was so uncool, dig?"

"I'm sorry," you say. "Do you speak English?"

"This is English, daddy-o," he says. "Don't you groove, baby? The cat you're after was here, but he split the scene. He said he was off to meet President Kennedy. You dig?"

You're beginning to understand, but the noise is getting to you. Head back to #5 to check out this clue.

#80. You've trailed Della Kitessen to a small country inn. It's a nice place to stop and eat, and that's about all you can do, because Della isn't here. Have a nice lunch, then head for #74.

#81. You're in Florida in 1968. The NASA technician was working on the capsule when it was stolen. Unfortunately, she can't tell you a lot.

"Whoever it was came up behind me," she says. "Then a bag was dropped over my head. By the time I got it off, the thief was already gone, and so was the capsule." She thinks for a moment. "But I did hear something — the crook mentioned going to a place that was made a state before 1860."

You thank her for her help and head for #133.

#82. You've landed in Hawaii in 1965. There are sun, sand, and surf galore — but not a trace of the crook you're seeking. Better head over to #21 and see why.

#83. You've found your way to a helicopter factory. Your head is obviously in a whirl, because there's no trace of Phil R. Yup. Better hop to #74 and discover the reason.

#84. The year is 1769, and you're in Delaware. Della where? No, Delaware — but nobody there. Better check things out at #21.

#85. You've reached California, and it's 1967. Things are changing radically in America — rock 'n' roll, the antiwar movement, and hippies are all in. It's a time when people are asking questions — so you should fit right in here when you ask a few of your own.

The computer on the Chronoskimmer bleeps to let you know it has some clues for you. Now you have a choice: You can question one of the people listed or you can investigate a place.

If you want to question:
The flower child — *go to #64*
The bomb shelter salesman — *go to #15*
The rock 'n' roller — *go to #129*

If you're ready to go to:
South Carolina in 1662 — *go to #44*
Washington in 1962 — *go to #137*
Florida in 1862 — *go to #121*

#86. You've reached the Iolani Palace, built in the nineteenth century for the Hawaiian king David Kalakaua. This is the only royal palace in America — but you're royally frustrated because Phil R. Yup isn't here. Better head on to #74 instead.

#87. You've arrived in Alabama in 1862. The Civil War is going strong and no one can answer your questions. Finally you give up and go to #21.

#88. You're in Vermont in 1968. One of the products Vermont is famous for is its high-quality marble. Mabel works at a marble quarry, getting the polished rock ready to ship all over the country. You ask her about the crook you're trailing.

"Yes, he was here," Mabel tells you. "Told me he was a time traveler, and that his next stop would be before the start of the Civil War. Did he escape from a mental hospital?"

You assure her he just has rocks in his head. Then you head back to #92 to check out this clue.

#89. The Chronoskimmer lands you in New York City. The year is 1863, so there are no skyscrapers yet, but it's a busy, crowded place. Immigrants from all over the world are coming to this country through the port of New York. It's truly a melting pot of nations.

The computer finishes its work and gives you a number of leads to follow. Now you have a choice: You can question one of the people listed or you can investigate a place.

If you want to investigate:
Postman Pat — go to #28
Rolling Ruby — go to #77
A Brother of the Footboard
  — go to #105

If you think the gang member went to:
Delaware in 1660 — go to #11

Alaska in 1960 — go to #52
Georgia in 1760 — go to #145

#90. You've landed in Hawaii in 1960. A young woman is handing out leis. Leis are necklaces made of flowers that are traditionally given to visitors to the islands as a form of greeting. You ask her about the woman you're after.

"Welcome to the island," the girl suggests, tossing a lei around your neck.

You realize that it's made not of pretty flowers but of a whole string of Venus flytraps, all snapping at you. The girl must be one of Carmen's gang! You finally manage to pull off the garland and throw it away. By then the girl has fled. Still, you know you're getting close to the crook. Head back to #130 to follow another of your leads.

#91. It's 1864 and the Civil War is raging. Kentucky never joined the rebel Southern states, but some people there still own slaves. President Lincoln freed the South's slaves with the Emancipation Proclamation last year, but it didn't apply to Kentucky. You're sad about this and turn to the on-board computer for clues.

Now you have a choice: You can question one of the people listed or you can investigate a place.

If you want to talk with:

The nurse — go to #115

The soldier — go to #38

The Underground Railroader — go to #66

If you're ready to catch the crook in:

Rhode Island in 1860 — go to #143

Connecticut in 1964 — go to #9

Nevada in 1967 — go to #151

#92. The Chronoskimmer stops, and you find yourself in 1968, in Vermont. Although it's the wrong season for skiing or for viewing colorful autumn leaves, there are many farms and enough maple syrup to cover a mountain of pancakes.

The computer buzzes to alert you that it has clues. Now you have a choice: You can question one of the people listed or you can investigate a place.

If you want to talk to:

Marble Mabel — go to #88

The ski instructor — go to #43

The maple tapper — go to #140

If you're ready to follow the thief to:
Pennsylvania in 1762 — go to #55
New York in 1867 — go to #18
Rhode Island in 1762 — go to #96

#93. Atlanta in 1760 is an elegant city, and Anne is a wealthy young lady you find at a society tea party. A bit different from the Tea Party they'll be having up in Boston in another few years.

You ask Anne about the crook you're chasing. "Her!" she says, full of scorn. "She tried to steal my jewelry. I tell you, she may be a female, but she is no lady!"

You use your best manners to thank her, and then you excuse yourself to return to #145.

#94. It's Connecticut in 1865. The man you want is usually out fishing in his small boat on Long Island Sound. Luckily for you, he's at home today, fixing a torn net. You talk to him about the thief you're after.

"She was here earlier," he tells you. "She said she had to go and meet the rebel chief Pontiac. I can't place the name — he must have fought for the South in the Civil War."

You tell him he's thinking of the wrong war, and you hurry back to #118 to check out this clue.

#95. You arrive at the shipyards in New London, on the Connecticut coast. The sailor you're searching for starts to run when he sees you. In fact, he runs right off the dock and into the water. You throw a life preserver over his shoulders and haul him onto the shore.

"You're all washed up," you tell him. Then you spot a sheet of paper in his cap. It's a list of names and addresses of Carmen's gang!

If you think the crook you're looking for is:

Della Kitessen — go to #13
Phil R. Yup — go to #83
Carmen Sandiego — go to #58
Casey Rah Sirah — go to #159
Skip Tumelu — go to #75
Claire Voyant — go to #147
Lucinda Boltz — go to #123
Homer DeBrave — go to #26

#96. The year is 1762, and Rhode Island is your destination. The state is famous for its chickens, known as Rhode Island Reds. Your face turns red when you discover you've made a mistake! Time to head for #21.

#97. You've trailed Della Kitessen to a barbecue party. Although there's lot to eat, Della is nowhere to be found. You grab a piece of fried chicken (or is it alligator?) and head off to #74.

#98. In 1969, Oklahoma is a state with a lot of oil wells. That oily crook you're after has given you the slip, though. Better move to #21 and find out why.

#99. Tombstone, got its name during the Wild West years, when plenty of rustlers, hustlers, and other outlaws ended up getting shot and buried here. But by 1962 there are no outlaws to be found. Tess is a waitress at the Last Chance Saloon. You ask her about the crook you're seeking.

"He was here, pardner," she tells you. "But he said he was taking the next stagecoach out of town. Said he was off to New Amsterdam. I never heard of that town — have you?"

It sure sounds familiar to you. You head back to #22 to check out your information and find where he could have gone.

#100. The Chronoskimmer has brought you to Virginia in 1862, the second year of the Civil War. In Richmond, the capital of the Confederate States of America, troops are massed under the command of General Robert E. Lee. Everybody seems to be armed and ready to fight, which makes you nervous. You don't carry a gun yourself, even in your dangerous job.

The on-board computer buzzes to let you know it has some information. Now you have a choice: You can question one of the people listed or you can investigate a place.

If you want to talk to:
Virginia from Virginia — go to #144
General Stonewall Jackson — go to #39
The Confederate senator — go to #108

If you think the thief has fled to:
Connecticut in 1662 — go to #67
New Hampshire in 1866 — go to #136
New York in 1666 — go to #14

#101. You've trailed Carmen Sandiego to a place in Florida that will one day be Cape Canaveral. There won't be any rockets launched from here, however, for almost a century. Carmen's not here. Better go to #74.

#102. The rocket man works at the White Sands Proving Ground, where space rocket engines are developed and tested. You ask him about the person you're after.

"I didn't see much," he tells you. "When we test our engines, a lot of dust whirls around, so all visitors here wear a protective mask. I did see brown hair, though. He also mentioned heading to somewhere to see a planetarium."

You blast off to #49 to check out this lead.

#103. The Democrat you find is campaigning for Lyndon B. Johnson for president in 1964. He hands you a campaign button that says ALL THE WAY WITH LBJ. You ask about the crook you're after.

"Sorry," the man tells you. "I've got a campaign to work on. That's all I can think about." You head back to #9 hoping for a better lead.

#104. You've followed Phil R. Yup to a Quaker meetinghouse. The group is having a religious meeting, and there's no sign at all of Phil. With a sigh, you head off to #74.

#105. Wondering what a Brotherhood of the Footboard is, you find yourself at a railway yard.

It's New York in 1863. The man you want to talk to is a locomotive engineer, and the Brotherhood is a new trade union he has joined. You ask him about the crook you're after.

"Didn't see anyone," he tells you. "I've got a train to run to Albany, and I can't talk. Clear the tracks!" This wasn't much help. You head back to #89, hoping for better luck on your next lead.

#106. You've arrived in Pennsylvania in 1869. A man named Henry J. Heinz started a food-packing business here this year, which sells grated horseradish. Someday it will become a huge company, but you can't wait that long, because the thief isn't here. Better pack off to #21.

#107. One of the most breathtaking sights in all of Arizona is the Grand Canyon. It's 1 mile deep, 4 to 18 miles wide, and 217 miles long. You strike up a conversation with the tour guide and ask her about the crook you're after.

"That sneak tried to steal a mule!" she tells you. "But good old Betsy kicked him in the pants. He got mad, and he said he was going somewhere else to celebrate Christmas."

You thank her for her help and head back to #22 to check out this clue.

#108. You've landed in Richmond, Virginia, in 1862. Richmond is the capital of the Confederate forces during the Civil War. You find a Confederate senator and ask him about the crook you're tailing.

"Any man who steals a horse should be horsewhipped himself, if you ask me," the senator growls. "I heard that that thief was off to a spot where he could see New Jersey across the river."

You thank him for his help and set off to #100 to check out this clue.

#109. As you arrive, Lester the blacksmith is pounding a piece of red-hot metal into a U shape. "Just finishing a horseshoe," he tells you. You ask him about the crook you're tracing.

"Yes, I saw the lady," he tells you. He plunges the red-hot shoe into a barrel of water to cool it down. Steam hisses out. "She said she was off to a place that became a state after 1840. Oh, and one more thing — she had me make her a little charm in the shape of an opossum. Said it was her favorite animal."

You thank him and set off back to #19 to work out what this all means.

#110. You've trailed Claire Voyant to Pearl Harbor. In the water is the sunken warship USS *Arizona*, left here as a memorial of the Japanese air attack that brought the United States into World War II. Your heart sinks, too, when you realize Claire's not there. Better give up and head for #74.

#111. You find Toby fishing in a quiet stream in the Georgia woods. He hasn't had a bite for a while, but that doesn't seem to bother him. You ask him if he's seen the man you're after.

"I remember he seemed in a hurry," Toby tells you. "Said he was off to see a Civil War battle. I had no idea what he was talking about." Then Toby jumps to his feet with a cry.

"Got a bite at last?" you ask.

"Sure have," he tells you, slapping his arm. "Pesky mosquito!"

You leave him to his fishing and head back to #139 to check out this clue.

#112. Illinois is a top pig-raising state, and "Hog" Wilde is the proud owner of a pig farm. He insists on showing you around as you ask about the crook you're after.

"I saw him earlier," he tells you. "He complained that he couldn't get any chocolate where he was going. Who needs chocolate when you can bring home top-quality bacon? Want to buy a pound?"

You politely refuse and head back to #116 to check out this clue.

#113. It's 1968, and you've landed in Florida. This state is noted for its beautiful offshore islands, known as the Keys. Many people earn a living taking tourists deep-sea fishing. The man you're after owns a big charter boat. He is mopping the deck as you approach. You ask about the crook you're chasing.

"That green-eyed so-and-so tried to steal my boat," he says angrily. "I'll give you whatever help I can. I remember hearing something about seeing a president before he's assassinated."

You thank the man and head back to #133.

#114. There are plenty of beavers, raccoons, and other animals in Louisiana that are prized for their fur. Trapper Jean spends most of his time in the wilderness catching and skinning such animals. You find him at a trading post where he has come to sell his furs. You ask about the crook you're trailing.

"She was here a while ago," he tells you. "Tried to steal one of my best otter skins! I soon sent her packing. She threatened to join something called the ASPCA to get back at me."

You thank him for his help and rush back to #16. Maybe you've got your crook trapped!

#115. It's 1864, and the Civil War is nearing its end. Still, there are plenty of nurses needed, you discover. The nurse you want to talk to is taking a well-earned break.

"I did see the man you're after," she tells you. "I think he had green eyes. But I didn't pay him much attention, because he didn't need any medical help."

You leave her to get on with her work, and head back to #91 to check out this clue.

#116. You've landed in the farm country of Illinois in 1969. Things are a lot quieter here than they were in nearby Chicago during the Democratic Convention of 1968. Suddenly your computer buzzes to let you know it has some leads. Now you have a choice: You can question one of the people listed or you can investigate a place.

If you want to talk to:
"Hog" Wilde — go to #112
Pru at the zoo — go to #160
The iron man — go to #51

If you're ready to move to:
New Hampshire in 1669 — go to #23
Oregon in 1868 — go to #124
Georgia in 1660 — go to #76

#117. In 1835 the Seminole Indians were supposed to move from Florida to reservations in the West, but they refused to go and fought U.S. troops for seven years.

Seminole Sam was a soldier in that war. He loves to tell tall tales about his army days. You ask him about the crook you're tailing.

"Cook?" he asks. "No, we didn't have no cook. Had to eat what we could find. I lived on snakes and scorpions for a year."

"Not cook," you reply. "A thief."

"Teeth?" he repeats. "Snakes ain't got teeth."

You try to end this conversation by saying, "Thanks."

"Fangs? Well, rattlesnakes sure do have fangs . . . "

You hurry back to #121 and hope that one of the other leads is of more use.

#118. You land in Connecticut in 1865. The Civil War is finally over, and a wave of relief and optimism has swept over the country. You won't feel relieved until you find your thief.

Your computer clicks, and spits out leads. Now you have a choice: You can question 👉

one of the people listed or you can investigate a place.

If you want to question:
The Courant *editor — go to #37*
The dressmaker — go to #170
The fisherman — go to #94

If you're ready to move on to:
Louisiana in 1763 — go to #16
Louisiana in 1663 — go to #138
Utah in 1963 — go to #69

#119. Betsy Ross lives in Philadelphia near the home of Ben Franklin. Betsy is only eight years old when you find her stitching away in her parents' front parlor. Hoping to sew up this case, you ask her about the crook you're chasing.

"He did stop by here," she tells you. "I recall he said he was interested in reading a book called *Little Women*. I'd never heard of it, but I advised him to go ask Ben Franklin. Ben is a printer, you know."

"He visited Ben's place before he came here," you say, "and he stole Ben's glasses." Thanking her for this clue, you decide to investigate more people and hurry back to #50.

#120. You've trailed Carmen Sandiego to a small silversmith's shop. Is she setting up another robbery? No — when you arrive at the store, you discover that it's gone out of business. You'd better move on to #74.

#121. The Chronoskimmer time machine has landed in Florida in 1862. Last year Florida became the third state to secede from the Union and join the Confederacy. Though someday Florida will be very valuable property, right now it's not much — mostly swamp and empty beaches.

You wait for the on-board computer to beep. This time it gives you a pretty short list.

If you want to investigate:

Seminole Sam— *go to #117*
The swamp rat — *go to #48*
The Southern senator — *go to #165*

#122. It's really warm in Hawaii, and you're hot on the trail of Carmen Sandiego. You've tracked her down to a banana plantation. Hawaii is famous for its luscious fruits, especially bananas and pineapples. You pick up a small bunch of bananas to munch for your lunch.

Suddenly Carmen springs out from behind a trailer piled high with pineapples. She hits the release on the trailer, and a bunch of prickly pineapples fall on you!

"Hah, gumshoe!" she taunts you. "I've given you the slip again."

That gives you an idea. You quickly peel a banana and toss the skin in front of Carmen. With a scream, she slips on the peel and falls. You slip a pair of handcuffs on her before she can get up again.

The police arrive to take Carmen away. In her pocket is a map of where she's hidden old New York City. Now it can be returned to its proper place and time. You call the Chief to tell him. "Great work, detective," he says happily. "Now head for the back of the book to check your score. I'll bet you earned yourself a promotion and bonus for this case!"

#123. You've trailed Lucinda Boltz to an auto repair shop in Hartford, Connecticut. But when you arrive, all you find are some cans of grease. She's obviously given you the slip. Better move on to #74.

#124. You've landed in Oregon. It's 1868, so this has been a state for only nine years. Oregon is noted for its salmon, but that's not the only thing that's fishy here. Swim off to #21 to find out what it is.

#125. You've trailed Skip Tumelu to Tallahassee, the capital of Florida. But he must have skipped the state, because he's nowhere in sight. You set your Chronoskimmer for #74 and zip over there.

#126. The Chronoskimmer places you in Philadelphia in the year 1769. You find Prudence studying hard. You have to admire her — in this era, women are not encouraged to go to school. Prudence agrees to take a short break to answer your questions.

"The woman you're looking for stopped by,"

she tells you. "She mentioned that she was off to visit one of the original thirteen colonies."

Thanking Prudence for her help, you leave her to her studies. Time to head back to #41 to check out this new information.

#127. You step through the door of a blues club. The lights are low, the talk quiet. On the stage is a singer with her guitar, singing a mournful song. The singer you want, however, is still in his dressing room. You make your way backstage. There you ask him about the crook you're looking for.

"Man, I don't have time for this," he tells you. "All I know is he said something about wanting to read about the first train robbery."

You leave him to his music and head back to #5 to check out this clue.

#128. You've landed in Philadelphia in 1762. The city has had oil-burning streetlights on several streets for five years now, thanks to Benjamin Franklin. The lamplighter's job is to light the oil lamps every evening at dusk. You watch him lift his long pole to carry a flame to the lamp wick. Then you question him about the thief you're trailing.

"I've got no time to talk," he tells you. "I can't leave the good people of Philadelphia in the dark, can I?"

You're the one who's left in the dark now. Return to #55, hoping for better luck with your next clue.

#129. It's 1967, and rock music is in this year. The top singers all have long hair, electric guitars, and vividly colored clothing. The singer you're looking for is dressed in a green velvet shirt and purple bell-bottom pants. You ask him about the crook you're after.

"Yeah, that chick was groovy," he says with a grin. "She said she wanted to steal a kiss from me. I gave her one for free. Said she was going to a Southern state from here."

You thank him and head back to #85 to check this out.

#130. As the Chronoskimmer comes to a halt, you're on a beautiful tropical beach in Hawaii, in 1960. This is more like it! If you weren't on a case, you could catch a few rays, get a cool drink, and relax. But instead, you set the computer working. There's a short list of possible clues.

If you want to check out:

The lei girl — go to #90
Hawaiian Ike — go to #25
The tour guide — go to #154

#131. You've arrived in Maine, in 1860. One thing about Maine hasn't changed over the years — the locals aren't much for talking. You can't get any answers to your questions, so you'd better move on to #21.

#132. It's the year 1669, and you are in New Hampshire. Nathaniel Morton is a writer visiting New Hampshire. He introduces himself and asks if you've read his latest book. He hands you a copy, and you look at the title:

New England's Memoriall, or a Brief Relation of the Most Memorable and Remarkable Passages of the Providence of God, Manifested to the Planters of New England in America; With Special Reference to the First Colony Therefore, Called New Plymouth.

"I think you need a shorter title," you tell him. "They'll have trouble fitting this one on the bestseller list."

"Yes, a black-haired man said the same thing," Morton tells you. "He also said he went somewhere where women can vote, but that doesn't sound right to me."

"Trust me, it is," you tell him. "But keep working on that title." You leave him to his thoughts and head back to #23 to check out this information.

#133. The Chronoskimmer lands you at Cape Kennedy, Florida, in the year 1968. The space race between the United States and the Soviet Union is at a crucial stage. NASA is ready to send up three astronauts in *Apollo 8*, the first spacecraft to orbit the Moon. But they won't be going anywhere if you can't get the capsule back!

The computer on the Chronoskimmer gives you a list of clues to check on, and some possible destinations where the crook may have fled. Now you have a choice: You can question one of the people listed or you can investigate a place.

If you want to question:

The boatman— go to #113

The NASA technician — go to #81

The Gator Aide — go to #7

If you think the thief escaped to:

Claire Voyant

Sex: Female
Hair: Brown
Eyes: Brown
Occupation: Former newspaper psychic for *The National Inquisitor.*
Favorite Food: Chinese
Weakness: She can't even predict tomorrow's date.
Favorite Animal: Opposum

Claire Voyant

Texas in 1963 — go to #149
New York in 1863 — go to #89
Virginia in 1763 — go to #32

#134. You've trailed Homer DeBrave to Mauna Loa, the largest volcanic mountain in the world. It's still active — the last time it erupted was in 1984. And since Homer isn't here, you might as well go to #74 before you get caught in a lava flow.

#135. You've landed in Connecticut, in 1964. The Republican is hard at work on a presidential campaign, trying to get Senator Barry Goldwater elected. You ask if he has seen the crook you're trailing. He hands you a campaign button. "I don't have time to talk to you," he says, "unless you're planning to vote for Goldwater!"

You haven't the heart to tell him that you're a little too young to vote. You head back to #9, hoping for better luck with your next lead.

#136. You've landed in New Hampshire, and the year is 1866. The Civil War is over, but a cholera epidemic is sweeping the country. You'd better get out of the way and head for #21.

#137. You've landed in 1962 in Washington State, the home of the world's largest hydroelectric facility, the Grand Coulee Dam. It produces a lot of electrical power, but you're not producing any clues. Better zip straight to #21.

#138. You've landed in Louisiana in 1663. Spanish explorers have traveled across it, but France will claim it when Robert de La Salle arrives here in 1682. At the moment, though, there are no European settlers. You may as well go to #21.

#139. You've landed in Georgia in 1662. There will be no European settlers in Georgia for another seventy-one years, so Native Americans still live here.

The on-board computer clicks, and gives you a list of clues to check out. Now you have a choice: You can question one of the people listed or you can investigate a place.

If you want to talk to:

Prudence — go to #17
William — go to #62
Toby — go to #111

If you're ready to move to:
Vermont in 1868 — go to #167
Michigan in 1862 — go to #46
Kentucky in 1864 — go to #91

#140. Vermont is famous for its maple syrup. The tapper's job is to drill a tap into each maple tree's trunk. As he hangs a pail from the tap to collect the sap, you ask him about the crook you're trying to nail.

"He sure had sticky fingers," the man tells you. "Tried to steal some maple sugar candy. I chased him away. He said he was off to see a historic play."

You thank the tapper and hop back to #92 to check this clue.

#141. You've trailed Phil R. Yup to an island in the Florida Keys. You know he loves bald eagles, but all you can find here are alligators. You decide to see what you can find out at #74.

#142. You've arrived in the colony of New York in 1664. At the Governor's Mansion, you find Richard Nicholls, the governor of New York. You ask about the crook you're trailing.

"Yes, I hope you can catch the scoundrel who stole my village," the governor tells you. "I spoke to my men, and one of them thought the thief was going on to see a king called Martin Luther."

You shake your head. "I think you mean a person called Martin Luther King, Jr."

"That's it!" he says, riding off. You race back to #12 to follow this lead.

#143. You've reached Rhode Island in the year 1860. Many rich people live in the town of Newport, so you'd think Carmen and her gang would be around, snooping for loot. But they're not here. Better get along to #21.

#144. You are in the state of Virginia in 1860. You meet a young girl named Virginia, who seems very excited by the upcoming Civil War. "Of course, the South will win," she insists. "We have the better soldiers. It's just a matter of time."

You decide not to tell her what will really happen. Instead, you ask about the crook who stole the general's horse.

"He must have been a Yankee!" she says. "I heard him say he was going to a time before any presidents had been assassinated. If you ask me, he's the one who should be shot!"

"Well, he'll spend a long time in jail," you promise her. "Just as soon as I catch him." You set off back to #100 to check out this lead.

#145. It's 1760, and you're in the prosperous colony of Georgia. Cotton is one of its most valuable crops, and a lot of African people have been brought here to work as slaves on the cotton plantations. It's a hard and cruel time for them.

Your computer suddenly flashes to let you know it has found some leads. Now you have a choice: You can question one of the people listed or you can investigate a place.

If you want to talk to:

The university student — go to #40
Anne from Atlanta — go to #93
The cotton picker — go to #161

If you're ready to travel to:
Kansas in 1865 — go to #19

New Jersey in 1965 — go to #153
Maryland in 1665 — go to #68

#146. You've reached one of the many beautiful beaches on Maui, Hawaii. If Lucinda Boltz is here, there's no way you'll ever find her: the place is packed with people sunbathing. With a sigh, you give up and head for #74.

#147. You've managed to trail Claire Voyant to a discotheque in 1967. The teenagers here are dancing some weird dances, with names like the Dog, the Monkey, the Pony, and the Frug. But you don't feel like dancing, because you can't find your thief. You'd best be off to #74 before someone asks you to dance the Watusi.

#148. It's 1664. The potter has a small shop not far from where old New York City stood before it was stolen. He is sitting at a potter's wheel, making drinking mugs out of clay and water. You ask him about the crook you're looking for.

"He stopped by earlier," the potter shouts above the noise of his wheel. "Told me he was off to see a super bowl. I tried to sell him one of my nice bowls, but he said he'd pass."

You decide not to tell him what the Super Bowl is — he's never even heard of football! You head back to #14 to check out this clue.

#149. You've landed in Texas in May of 1963. In November, President John F. Kennedy will be gunned down in Dallas, but there's nothing much happening now. Better move to #21.

#150. You've trailed Della Kitessen to a luau — a Hawaiian feast that usually centers around a pig roasted in a deep pit. Sounds like the kind of pig-out Della loves, but she's nowhere to be seen. The food smells great, but you're working, so go to #74.

#151. The year is 1967, and you've landed in Nevada. It's the gambling capital of America, but if you bet that the crook is here, you'd lose your money. Take a trip to #21.

#152. You've trailed Casey Rah Sirah to a musical appreciation society. But you don't appreciate what you find, which is just a string quartet and an audience. There's no sign of Casey, so you have to change your tune and go to #74.

#153. You've arrived in New Jersey, at the popular Palisades Amusement Park, in the year 1965. But you don't feel like going on any of the rides, since there's no sign of the crook you're after. You give up and go to #21 to find out why.

#154. You're in Hawaii in 1960. You find the tour guide leading a party to Hawaii Volcanoes National Park. You tag along, and ask him about the crook you're after.

"I haven't seen anyone at all," he tells you. But then he pulls a gun from his pocket, and you realize that he's really one of Carmen's thugs!

Quickly you grab a coconut from one of the tourists and use it to knock the gun from the guide's hand. Then you use a lei to tie up his hands. "You'll look pretty when the police arrive," you tell him.

You're obviously getting very close to Carmen

now, so head back to #130 to check one of the other leads.

#155. The year is 1869, and you've landed in Iowa. A woman named Arabella Mansfield has just been accepted to practice law, making her the first woman lawyer in the United States. But you don't need a lawyer — you need a crook. Try heading for #21.

#156. The Chronoskimmer brings you to South Carolina in the year 1963. After a lot of civil rights protests, the state has finally opened its colleges to Black students. But since you can't find any clues here, you'd better go to #21.

#157. You've trailed Claire Voyant to a big piece of swampland in Florida, which she's trying to sell to a couple of gullible buyers. "I predict that one day this will be a popular tourist resort," she tells them.

"And I predict you're going to jail, Claire," you tell her.

She tries to run, but she slips and splashes down in the swamp. Speaking of splashing down, you find the map of where she has hidden the stolen space capsule in her purse. The police lead her away in handcuffs, and you call the Chief.

"Excellent work!" he tells you happily. "Well, head for the back of the book to check your score and to see if you've earned your raise and promotion!"

#158. The Chronoskimmer has landed you in North Carolina in 1669. This colony was founded only sixteen years ago by settlers moving south from Virginia. Unfortunately, the thief you're after has moved, so you'd better go to #21.

#159. You've tailed Casey Rah Sirah to a TV store, where you thought he'd be watching a boxing match on TV. The winner is Muhammad Ali, who just changed his name from Cassius Clay. Maybe Casey changed his name, too, because he's nowhere to be seen. You go down for the count and head for #74.

#160. Pru is a keeper at the Lincoln Park Zoo in Chicago. As she feeds the seals, you ask her about the crook you're trailing.

"I haven't seen anyone fishy here at all," she says, tossing another herring to the seals. "I've been too busy with my work."

You leave her to it as you head back to #116.

#161. You make your way out to the cotton fields. In the broiling sun, African slaves stoop low over the rows of cotton plants. You find the worker you're after and start talking to him while he swiftly plucks cotton.

"Yessir," the slave tells you, "the woman you're looking for was here. But she said she was going on to a place that had been made a state this past year."

Just then you are interrupted by the overseer, a harsh man who keeps the slaves hard at work. You wish you could give him a taste of that whip he carries, but you know the rules — you're not supposed to interfere in the past. You're forced to leave the slave to his work, even though it hurts you to do so.

You head back to #145, hoping this clue means you can get out of this time and place as fast as possible.

#162. The hunter they call Pierre the Bear claims to have killed many grizzly bears. You can believe it — he's so huge, he could probably eat them for breakfast! You ask him about the woman you're after.

"I remember she mentioned liking coyotes better than grizzly bears," he tells you. "But that's all."

You thank him and head back to #16 to check this clue out.

#163. You've reached Texas in 1969. There's no one here to help you. You'd better travel to #21.

#164. You've tracked Skip Tumelu to a woodworker's shop in Philadelphia in the year 1743. The furniture made here will be worth a fortune in the twentieth century. But Skip isn't here, so you pack up and go to #74.

#165. You arrive at the home of the Southern senator. Just as you do, you see a man running from the house. The senator appears in the doorway and yells, "Stop, thief!"

Instantly, you set off after the crook. With a tackle that would make a football coach smile, you bring the man down. He's one of the thugs Carmen sometimes hires, and he has stolen money from the senator's house. Also in his pocket is something that interests you a lot more: a sheet of paper with the names and addresses of Carmen's gang on it!

If you think that the thief who stole the *Apollo 8* capsule is:

Carmen Sandiego — *go to #101*
Skip Tumelu — *go to #125*
Casey Rah Sirah — *go to #60*
Claire Voyant — *go to #157*
Lucinda Boltz — *go to #24*
Phil R. Yup — *go to #141*
Della Kitessen — *go to #97*
Homer DeBrave — *go to #72*

#166. You've landed in Michigan, in the year 1861. Four of the five Great Lakes border this state, and you feel like you're bordering on insanity. There's nobody here, so you head for #21.

#167. You've reached the Green Mountains of Vermont in 1868. You feel pretty green yourself when you realize it's the wrong place to be. Better travel to #21.

#168. You trail Homer DeBrave to a field where he's showing some locals how to play baseball. But they keep getting the rules confused with an older game called rounders, which is very similar.

When Homer sees you, he makes a run for it. You grab the ball he's left behind and throw it with all your might. It hits him on the back of the head and he slumps to the ground.

"Strike!" you yell. "And you're out!"

When the police arrive, they find Traveller by Homer's time machine, quietly munching grass. They promise to return him to Robert E. Lee, and you call the Chief to tell him the case is over.

☞

"Wonderful work," the Chief says happily. "Better move on to the back of the book and see if you've earned that promotion and bonus!"

#169. In a small farmhouse just outside of town, you find the nester. That's a name given to someone who moves into an abandoned building and makes it his home. This nester has worked hard to make a go of this small farm. You ask him about the woman you're after.

"She stopped by here to see if I'd found any opossums," he tells you. "Said she was awfully fond of them. But I haven't seen any."

You thank him for his help and head back to #19 to check out the clue.

#170. It's 1865, and you find Dorothy the dressmaker in her small shop, cutting lace to trim a dress. You ask about the woman you're trying to trace.

"She was in here," Dorothy replies. "She mentioned that she was going to a place that had once been a French colony. Then she tried to steal one of my dresses when she left."

"Sounds like one of Carmen's gang, all right," you say and return to #118 to check out this lead.

SCORING CHART

Add up all your travel points (you did remember to mark one point for each time you moved to a new number, didn't you?). If you have penalty points for trying to arrest the wrong person, add those in too. Then check your score against the chart below to see if you earned a raise and a promotion.

0 – 17:
You really couldn't have solved the cases in so few points. Either you're boasting about your skills, or you're actually working for Carmen's gang. Be honest and try again — if you dare!

18 – 40:
Super sleuth! You work very well and don't waste time. Well done — you deserve the new rank and the big fat bonus you'll get next payday.

41 – 60:
Private eye material! You're a good, steady worker, and you always get your man (or woman). Still, there's room for improvement, so try again and see if you can get that promotion.

61 – 80:

Detective first class. You're not a world-famous private eye yet, but you're getting there. Try again and see if you can move up a grade or two!

81 – 100:

Rookie material. You're taking too long to track down the crooks. Next time they'll get away from you. Try a little harder and see if you're better than this!

Over 100:

Are you sure you're really cut out to be a detective? Maybe you'd be better off finding an easier job — a janitor for Acme, maybe? Still, if you're determined to be a detective, give it another try. Better luck next time.